The Hunt

Hugh Ryan

SCHOLASTIC INC.

To Jason & Tim — creators of
the best scavenger hunt ever.
— H.R.

ISBN 978-0-545-46306-5

12 11 10 9 8 7 6 5 4 3 2 1   12 13 14 15 16 17/0

Printed in the U.S.A.   40
First Scholastic printing, September 2012

CHAPTER
ONE

Ray Fong noticed the shoe flying at his head just in time to duck behind his lunch tray. It hit with a heavy metal *clang*—it must have been one of those new robotic shoes the Tech students had invented—then smashed to the ground in a puff of smoke. Carefully, he peeked out from behind his temporary shield.

Two juniors were fighting Crane-style atop a nearby table, trading punches too fast for the eye to follow. As Ray watched, a low sweep kick knocked one to the ground, sending his other shoe to join the first at Ray's feet. The assembled freshmen cheered, but Ray just shook his head.

"It's going to be one of *those* days," he mumbled, as he tried to make his way through the crowded cafeteria to the lunch line. It wouldn't have been so bad if two robotic armies weren't battling in one corner, making a quarter of the cafeteria unusable.

He shouldn't have been surprised. Today was the Hunt, the biggest, most important day of the year at St. Perfidious Yearling Academy. Everyone was showing off, which was saying a lot, since St. Perfidious was pretty crazy on a normal day. As the most prestigious (and difficult) spy school in the world, its student body was known for their amazing skills, their outrageous exploits, and their intense competitiveness. Everyone wanted to be the best.

Except maybe Ray. Ray was a pretty normal kid. Well, as close as you could get to normal at St. Perfidious. He was tall and gangly, with olive-colored skin and coal black hair. He did fine in his classes, but not spectacularly. He enjoyed a few extracurricular activities (knitting club and amateur bomb squad, to be exact), but he spent most of his time by himself or with a few friends. Ray liked to watch and observe, and if other kids mistook that for being shy, it didn't really bother him.

Now that the fight was finished and it was safe to use his tray for its intended purpose, Ray turned his attention to lunch. He snagged a burger from the grill and poured french fries around it. Then he spotted the orange Jell-O, his favorite dessert! They usually served it only on Tuesdays, but it must have been put out especially for the Hunt.

"Nom!" he said, as he speared some with his fork.

"Ow!" yelled the Jell-O. Ray blinked. The Jell-O blinked back. Ray leaned in closer.

"Oh, sorry, Heather," he apologized to the girl cleverly disguised as dessert, but she only jiggled.

"Shhh!" she hissed.

It was all too much for Ray. Everyone was trying to impress the teachers in hopes of being chosen to join the Hunt. But didn't they know that the teachers had already made their choices? Besides, showing off wouldn't impress them. Ippon Sensei, head of the Martial Arts program at St. Perfidious, always told her students that fighting should be your last resort. Did those two juniors really think she'd be impressed by their careless battle? And M. Masque, the school's disguise expert, always said to never waste a good outfit. Ray wasn't going to be fooled by an orange Jell-O disguise again—that was for sure.

"I heard Kim and Ken Cohen are definitely going to be in the Hunt," said the girl behind Ray in line.

"Duh!" said her friend. "They totally ruled that surprise mission they went on. I hope *I* get to be in the Hunt next year."

The Hunt, the Hunt, the Hunt, thought Ray. *Is that all anyone can talk about?* (The answer, by the way, was yes: That was all any student at St. Perfidious could talk about that day. The Hunt, for those who haven't read *St. Perfidious: A History of the World's Greatest Spy School in Seventy-two Volumes,* was a tradition from the very first days of the academy. Five trophies, representing the five specialties at St. Perfidious—Martial Arts, Disguise, Strategy, Technology, and Stealth—were hidden throughout the campus. The head of each specialty chose two students to compete to find them in the most difficult scavenger hunt ever made. No student had ever found all five trophies except for Agent 4, the bubbly master spy in charge of Stealth. How she'd managed it was a mystery to this day.)

"Dear students." Headmaster Cornelius Booker's voice crackled over the PA system. "Please make your way calmly—CALMLY—to the main quad, where we will announce the names of the students chosen to participate in the Hunt this year."

The cafeteria exploded into chaos before Headmaster Booker had even finished. All of the students were trying to get through the main doors at the same time. Ray grabbed his burger and headed for the smaller side exit, which led away from the quad and deeper into the tunnels where most of St. Perfidious was located. The aboveground portions of the school were a fully functional, but completely fake, boarding school. All the real stuff was hidden way underground. Ray knew he wasn't going to be chosen as a Hunter, and so he had planned a busy day. While the rest of the students were watching or helping with the Hunt, he was going to take advantage of all the facilities that usually had long waiting lists: the antigravity chamber, the rocket firing range, the student-driver helicopters.

"Aren't you headed the wrong way?" a woman's voice interrupted Ray's thoughts. He looked up to find a heavily burdened Agent 4 coming down the hallway toward him. Her green and blue outfit perfectly matched the mysterious bags and folders she was carrying. That was Agent 4 for you: She always looked good, even in the middle of a mission. Her personal motto was "Looking good, spying good."

"No," said Ray. "I'm headed down to the dive room."

Agent 4 crinkled her cute little brow at him. "Don't you want to see if you've been chosen for the Hunt?"

Ray shook his head.

"It's cool," he said. "I know I'm not one of the Hunters."

"How do you know that?" asked Agent 4. Her voice was perky and bright, as though by tone alone she could convince Ray that he had a chance of being chosen.

"It's obvious," said Ray. "I'm not mad!" He rushed to explain. "It's just, well, you're going to pick Tanya Jones and Eric Appleton. Right?"

Agent 4 pulled back in surprise. "Why . . . why do you say that?" she stuttered. Ray had her full attention now.

"Easy," said Ray. "They're two of the top students in the school. They're both shoo-ins for the Hunt."

"Okay," said Agent 4, who was clearly thinking hard now. "But how do you know I'll choose them?"

"In class, if someone gives an answer that's, like, mostly correct, but not completely, you always call on Tanya or Eric to correct them. So they must be your favorites—and with good reason. They totally deserve to be in the Hunt."

Ray didn't want Agent 4 to think he was angry about not being chosen. He was just being practical. Agent 4 looked at him for a long time, tapping one perfectly manicured nail against her lower lip.

It was as though she was seeing him for the first time, and it made Ray very uncomfortable. He was much more accustomed to not being seen.

"Um, so, I guess . . . I'm gonna go," he mumbled. "Have fun at the Hunt!"

Agent 4 didn't move. After a second, she smiled.

"Well, I can't stop you," she said. "But could I at least ask you for some help?"

She thrust a large blue duffel bag at him. "I'm already late, and the Hunt can't get started until I arrive. Can you carry this for me? It'll only take a few minutes."

"Sure," said Ray. He was in no hurry. The Hunt usually took eight or ten hours, so he had all the time in the world to fire rockets and pilot helicopters. He picked up the bag and hurried after Agent 4, not knowing that his day—and, in fact, his whole life—was about to change forever.

CHAPTER TWO

In a dark gym in the deepest part of St. Perfidious, Tanya Jones stood absolutely still, balanced atop a tall pillar. The gym was filled with obstacles and strange contraptions for mock fights. She was barefoot and wearing simple black sparring pants with a long-sleeved purple T-shirt. Somewhere in the distance, she heard a quiet whining sound, like the humming of a laptop. It was growing louder by the second. Her heart started to race.

Be still, she told herself. Ippon Sensei always said that stillness was a warrior's first weapon. She heard the old woman's voice in her mind: *"Let them come to you."*

The sound had become a roaring, tearing thing. Tanya's eyes were drawn to the double doors at the other end of the gym, which exploded outward as a low black motorcycle burst through them. The noise of its engine filled the room, and it was all Tanya could do not to run. She knew as long as she stayed still, she would be nearly invisible. She was wearing black, the room was dark, and she was high up, out of sight.

Her opponent popped a wheelie on his bike. He knew she was here somewhere, and he was trying to scare her. But all it did was bring him closer to her. She estimated the distance between them. She had to time this perfectly.

Three, two . . . one!

She leaped down from the pillar as the motorcycle shot by her. Instinctively, the driver pulled to the side to avoid her, which sent him careening into one of the trenches that ran through the gym floor. They were great for Stealth training exercises, and for causing motorcycles to crash. Her opponent landed heavily on the ground as the motorcycle went belly-up in the hole.

"Ha!" she yelled. "Got you!"

Tanya dropped into a fighting crouch, ready to spar. But her opponent lay where he had fallen.

"Eric?" she called out. "Are you okay?"

There was no response. Nervously, Tanya crept forward.

"Hey, man, come on. You're scaring me. Eric!"

Tanya was standing over Eric now. She'd torn his helmet off, and his curly brown hair was covering most of his face. He was breathing, but he didn't seem to be conscious.

"I'm going for he—" Tanya started to say, when suddenly Eric's leg snapped out and knocked her to the ground.

"Got *you*!" he yelled, as he jumped on top of her.

"Eric Appleton, you're a cheater!"

Locked together in a fierce battle, they rolled this way and that across the gym. Tanya tried to head butt Eric, but he blocked with his forearm. Eric yanked her hair, but Tanya tickled until he let go. He grabbed her wrists in a wrestling move known as the Eight-Armed Octopus, but she countered with the Hungry Hippo, and broke away.

In a flash, Tanya was on her feet and running. If she could get some distance—but no, Eric was right behind her. He was so close that she could feel his breath on the back of her neck. He leaped at her, but Tanya crumpled into a ball, and Eric went sailing over her . . . face-first into the pillar. There was a terrible *crack!*

"Eric?" said Tanya, carefully staying out of reach. "Are you okay?"

"No," said Eric through gritted teeth. "I think my jaw is broken!"

Tanya rushed toward him, then paused. "If you're faking this, I'm never going to forgive you."

But Eric was in too much pain to respond. Tanya ran to the wall and pressed the emergency assistance button. St. Perfidious had one of the best infirmaries in the world, and they'd have Eric patched up in no time. But today, no time wouldn't be soon enough.

"Eric, we're going to miss the Hunt!" said Tanya sadly. It started in fifteen minutes, and no miracle of modern medicine would have Eric fixed in time.

"No, we're not," he whispered, though every

word hurt him. "You know Agent 4 is going to pick you. You have to go. I'll be okay."

"I can't leave you like this!" Tanya protested.

The double doors of the gym banged open. Two students in medical scrubs entered, carrying a stretcher between them.

"I'll be fine. Go!"

But still, Tanya hesitated. Eric was her best friend—and her biggest rival at St. Perfidious. Everyone knew they were going to be chosen to be Hunters. They'd been planning for this all year. It was the only way, they'd decided, to figure out which one of them was the better spy.

"Go!" Eric yelled, even though it hurt him. "Now that I can't compete, someone's got to win."

He winked at her, and Tanya couldn't help but smile. She started to say something, but Headmaster Booker's voice was suddenly blasting from the loudspeakers. The Hunt was starting! Tanya gave Eric a quick (but gentle!) hug as they loaded him onto a stretcher. Then she started running. If she wasn't there when they announced the Hunters, she'd be disqualified.

Luckily, everyone else was already at the quad, so Tanya made good time running through the halls. Once she was aboveground, she raced through the gardens, leaped over a groundskeeper planting flowers (scaring him half to death), and made it to the quad just in time to hear Headmaster Booker finish his speech about the history of the Hunt. He was standing at a podium beneath a statue of himself. To his right was a long table, at which sat the other four teachers of St. Perfidious Yearling Academy: Ippon Sensei (Martial Arts), Dr. O (Technology), Agent 4 (Stealth), and M. Masque (Disguise). At least, Tanya was pretty sure that the giant toy robot on the table was Professor Masque in disguise. Some days it was hard to tell.

The entire student body of St. Perfidious seemed to be standing on the grassy quad in front of the teachers. Tanya joined the back of the crowd to listen to the rest of the headmaster's speech.

"Those of you chosen to participate in the Hunt join the ranks of some of our most illustrious alumni, like our own Agent 4, the only student ever to find all five trophies on her own!"

The crowd burst into applause. Agent 4 was a living legend at St. Perfidious.

"A-gent 4! A-gent 4!" the students chanted. Slowly, she made her way to the stage.

"Thank you all." She smiled sweetly. "It is my honor to read you the rules of the Hunt."

Agent 4 cleared her throat and pulled out a slim leather-bound book from her pocket. She flipped the pages.

"Rule number one: Five trophies will be hidden on the grounds of St. Perfidious Academy. Each one represents one of the five disciplines of study: Martial Arts, Stealth, Disguise, Technology, and Strategy. Be warned, none of these trophies will be easy to get! Hunters will be pushed to their limits. Just so you all know, this is what the trophies look like."

Agent 4 pulled a small silver cube, about the size of a baseball, out of her pocket and showed it off to the assembled students. Then she placed it on the podium.

"Ohhhh!" said the crowd.

"Rule number two," continued Agent 4. "Each teacher will choose two students to be Hunters. These Hunters will compete to find the five trophies. Each Hunter will be given one of these."

Agent 4 held up a gray glove. The palm and fingers sparkled from the miniature circuit boards sewn into it.

"Upon finding one of the trophies," said Agent 4, "the Hunter will touch it with their glove. This will register the trophy as found, and their name will be placed on the leaderboard next to the appropriate discipline."

Agent 4 pointed to the giant screen that sat behind the teachers' table. There were five rows, one for each field of study at St. Perfidious. Each had a blank space next to it just waiting to be filled with a Hunter's name.

"Now," Agent 4 said with a giant smile on her face, "comes the moment you've all been waiting for. I will announce the Hunters!"

Somehow, Tanya found herself standing just a few feet away from Agent 4. She didn't even remember worming her way through the crowd.

She'd been waiting all year for this moment, and now it was finally here. She stood on tiptoes, as if being an inch closer to Agent 4 would make any difference.

"The first two Hunters are . . ." Agent 4 paused for dramatic effect. "Kim and Ken Cohen!"

No surprise there, thought Tanya, as the twins walked up to the podium to receive their gloves. The Cohen twins had been at the top of their class even before they wowed the school in a surprise mission last year. Tanya was betting that they would be her toughest competition in the Hunt. But she wasn't *that* worried.

Agent 4 read down the list. There were a few surprises—Tanya had never even heard of Alexa de Beauxregard, and up until Agent 4 said his name, she'd thought Maxwell Melina was still in the hospital recovering from an unfortunate competitive musical chairs incident.

When her own name was called second to last, Tanya lifted her head high and half walked, half jogged to Agent 4's side.

"I chose you myself," said Agent 4 quietly, as

she put the glove on Tanya's hand. "You and Eric Appleton. So make me proud!"

Tanya's heart sank. No one had told Agent 4 about the accident!

"Eric can't!" she blurted out. "He's injured!"

Quickly, Tanya explained what had happened. The crowd was growing impatient, waiting for the final name.

"Oh dear," said Agent 4, when Tanya finished. "I'll have to choose someone else."

Her voice seemed far away, as though her mind were elsewhere. As Tanya watched, Agent 4 stared out at the students in front of her. The crowd grew quiet, waiting for the final name. Tanya was pretty sure she would choose Xerxes Papadalos, the Greek prince, or maybe that freshman boy who was only 3'4" tall. He could sneak up on anyone!

"The final Hunter will be . . ." Agent 4 paused. She opened her mouth, started to say something, then paused again. Suddenly, she swung around in a circle and pointed at a boy half-hidden in the shadow of the judges' table.

"Ray Fong!"

CHAPTER THREE

Ray couldn't believe what he'd just heard. For a second, he was convinced it was a dream. Or, rather, a nightmare. Did Agent 4 really just call his name?

"Ray?" Agent 4 repeated, looking right at him and gesturing with the final Hunter's glove. *His* Hunter's glove, he reminded himself. He still couldn't believe it was actually happening. *He* was a Hunter.

Wait, thought Ray. *What if this isn't really happening?*

He grinned and pinched his hand as hard as

he could, certain that he'd found the answer and would wake up back in his dorm room. But nothing happened, except now his hand hurt.

In a daze, Ray walked to the podium. He couldn't help but notice that some of the other Hunters—okay, *most* of the other Hunters—were looking at him strangely. There were always a few long shots in the Hunt, students who weren't at the top of their classes and hadn't won big awards. But usually they had some unique skill that offset everything else, like Erica and her robotic arms. She had been an obvious choice for Dr. O. But Ray himself was just . . . average.

There goes my chance to play in the zero-gravity chamber, he thought as Agent 4 fitted the glove over his hand. She beamed a perky smile at him, but Ray didn't have the heart to return it. The other teachers were applauding, but he couldn't meet their eyes. He'd had such a good day planned, and now he was going to miss it all to participate in a game that he would never win! Agent 4 had chosen the wrong person. This was all so totally unfair.

"Congratulations to this year's Hunters!" Agent

4 yelled into the microphone. The crowd went wild. A large group of the biggest boys in school began to chant, "Ken! Ken! Ken!" while overhead a robotic plane spelled out TANYA RULES in purple smoke.

It isn't hard to tell who the favorites are in this game, Ray thought to himself. *No one's chanting my name.* He cocked his ear to listen to the crowd and confirm his no-supporters status.

"Goooooo, Ray!"

Ray was shocked to hear his name among the others. He looked into the crowd and saw a long line of girls from his grade doing the wave. As each girl raised her arms, she yelled his name. Ray couldn't help but smile. Maybe he did have some fans. . . .

Suddenly, a thrumming noise filled the quad, as though an invisible giant had struck a gong the size of a mountain. The crowd quieted. The Hunters flexed their gloves and sized up their competition, all except for Ray, who was staring at his feet. There was a long pause.

Finally, Agent 4 leaned in toward the

microphone. "That was the bell. The Hunt has begun. Go!"

Ray thought it had been noisy before, but now the crowd truly showed how loud they could get. The roar of excitement was nearly deafening. His fellow Hunters were already racing out of the quad. As he watched, Lisa Terrington, a junior who had been chosen to participate in the Hunt by Headmaster Booker, touched a silver button at the center of her backpack.

Ka-chung!

Four bright silver wheels tore through the fabric of Lisa's backpack. She unzipped it the rest of the way, revealing a small motorized scooter. She tore the last scraps of the backpack off the device and hopped on. Before Ray could even straighten up, she was just a tiny dot in the distance. Clearly, she had a plan.

In fact, all the other Hunters seemed to be moving with great purpose. Kim and Ken Cohen whispered a few words to each other and then split up, moving quickly but calmly toward . . . *something*. Bishop McMath Ryan, the only freshman in this year's Hunt, was busy brushing a thin layer of goo all over himself. Ray wasn't certain what the stuff was, but it seemed to make him incredibly sticky. As Ray watched, a petal flowing in the wind brushed the edge of Bishop's sleeve and was caught. Once he was fully covered in goo, Bishop ran headfirst into the nearby bushes. Within seconds, he was completely covered in leaves and dirt, rendering him totally invisible.

He must be one of Professor Masque's, Ray thought to himself. Dimly, he was aware that he should be doing something, but he had no idea what that something was. He'd never once imagined being a Hunter, and so he had no strategy worked out. Instead, he fell back to his usual routine: watching and listening.

One by one the other Hunters disappeared, and most of the students went with them. Some went to follow their favorites. Others headed to the underground cafeteria, where the school's security cameras would be patched into giant flat screens, guaranteeing no one would miss a moment of the Hunt. Those who wanted to watch privately could log in using their Wearable Apparatus for Tracking, Cracking, and Hacking, or WATCH. A WATCH was issued to every student on the first day of class. A select few students were assisting with the Hunt, and had left to do the mysterious (but important) tasks that had been assigned to them. They wore bright blue shirts and matching headbands.

Maybe I should follow one of them? Ray thought, but before he could make up his mind, they were all gone.

In fact, everyone was gone. The once-crowded quad was completely deserted. Aside from the teachers, there was no one in sight.

Ray remembered a nightmare he'd once had. In it, he showed up to school only to discover he was supposed to take a final exam in a class he'd never been to! Midway through the test, he'd realized he was wearing only underwear. Things had gotten even worse when twenty armed polar bears invaded the classroom, intent on making a "Ray Fong cheesecake" (whatever that was). When he woke up, Ray discovered that he'd chewed up half his pillow in his sleep.

And he *still* felt better then than he did right now.

"What do I do now?" Ray wondered out loud, more to himself than to anyone else.

"You try to find the trophies," answered Agent 4, startling Ray. He had been so deep in his thoughts he hadn't even noticed when she walked up to him.

"But I'm not cut out for this!" said Ray. As soon as he said it, he wished he could take it back. Being chosen for the Hunt was an honor. Tons of other kids would have killed to be in his shoes.

Agent 4 gave him a long look. Ray blushed. In fact, he blushed so hard he could feel waves of heat radiating off his face. It was like having the sun for a head. But he couldn't look away. Finally, Agent 4 broke the silence.

"Maybe you're not," she agreed. She shook her head sadly and walked back to the table where the other teachers were seated. She said something too quiet for Ray to hear, and suddenly all the teachers were looking at him.

Please, Ray thought to himself, *let just one armed polar bear appear. Just one!*

But he was awake, and this was reality, and there were no armed polar bears coming to his rescue.

Ray decided he would give up. No one could *force* him to look for the trophies. And even if they tried, he could just say he was looking for clues in the antigravity chamber. Ray sniffled and told himself he wasn't going to cry. He turned his back on the teachers and the leaderboard, and began to walk away. The sun beat down on the back of his neck, and it felt like the hard stare of Agent 4.

As he stepped off the quad and onto the small brick path that would bring him to the hidden entrance to the rest of St. Perfidious, he couldn't help but look back. He wasn't sure, but he thought Agent 4 was watching him go.

She knows I'm quitting, he realized. But she wasn't going to stop him. Feeling about two inches tall, Ray turned around and left.

Or rather, he started to, but something caught his eye. He turned back and stared at the quad, trying to figure out what it was.

There!

It was the sun glinting off the fake trophy Agent 4 had shown the crowd. She'd left it on the podium. That wasn't like her. Agent 4 was normally neat and organized to a fault. If she'd left something behind, it was on purpose. What was it she always said in class? *"Sometimes, the best place to hide something is in plain sight. No one ever suspects it."*

Ray was flat-out running before he'd even made the decision to move. If he was wrong, this was going to be very embarrassing. But if he was right . . .

He slapped his gloved hand down over the silver cube. The giant gong sounded again. Ray looked up and saw his name appear on the leaderboard next to the word "Stealth." The teachers began applauding wildly. Ray was so surprised he nearly dropped the trophy.

"Congratulations!" said Agent 4, who was once again smiling her perkiest smile at him. "You now hold the St. Perfidious Yearling Academy record for the fastest find of all time—six minutes, four seconds."

It was all Ray could do not to jump up and down with joy. Agent 4 lifted an eyebrow and looked at him curiously.

"There are four more, you know. Get going!"

Ray ran.

CHAPTER FOUR

As soon as Agent 4 announced that the Hunt had begun, Tanya was off and running. She barreled straight into the crowd and within seconds was completely hidden by the bodies of her classmates. Quickly, she pulled off her long-sleeved purple T-shirt to reveal a plain black one underneath. Then she removed the wig she'd been wearing all semester, transforming her long blond hair into a short brown ponytail. With a pair of fake glasses and a baseball cap, her disguise was complete. If any of the other Hunters thought they could follow her and find the trophies that way, they had another thing coming!

Tanya had been planning for this day all year. In her opinion, Eric was the only *real* competition. Now that he was out of the game, she was certain she'd get all the trophies herself. She had a simple plan. (She liked simple plans—simple, direct, and effective, like she was herself.) She'd researched the past ten Hunts, and discovered a few small but important facts that would give her an edge over the other players. These were:

1. The Strategy trophy was always found last, which made sense because Headmaster Booker was a total spy genius. This was even more impressive because he told everyone that it was hidden in the exact same place every year. There was no point in looking for that trophy until she had all the others.

2. The Stealth and Disguise trophies were usually puzzles of some kind. The hardest part was cracking the code, but once you did, they weren't hard to get.

3. The Martial Arts and Tech trophies were usually pretty easy to locate. The hard part was getting past the guards and traps that Ippon Sensei and Dr. O had built.

Tanya decided to go after the Martial Arts and Tech trophies first, since they were the easiest to find. She was worried someone else might get them while she was puzzling through one of the others. And the whole time she was working on the first trophies, she could be thinking about where the others were hidden. Logical reasoning was one of Tanya's many skills.

With all this in mind, Tanya had spent the last week tracking Ippon Sensei, which was much harder than it sounded. Although she was an old woman, Sensei moved with the speed and grace of a young cheetah. To slow her down, Tanya had stolen all her shoes and replaced them with ones that were just slightly too small. They were close enough to her old pairs that she wouldn't notice, but uncomfortable enough that they made her walk at a normal human pace.

Thus, Tanya had been able to follow Sensei to a little-used elevator at the very back of the main library. The sign on the door said COLD STORAGE — NO ENTRANCE, but that didn't stop Sensei from going in night after night. Tanya didn't know what else was down there, but she was certain her first trophy was.

Luckily, on the day of the Hunt, not even the most dedicated students would be in the library. Indeed, when Tanya made it to the large glass doors, she could see that there was but one lonely librarian inside, and his eyes were glued to a monitor on which he was no doubt watching the Hunt.

As Tanya pulled open the heavy glass doors, a gong sounded.

No way! she thought. It had to be some kind of mistake. No one could have found one of the trophies already. Quickly, she typed a few commands into her WATCH. Her eyes nearly bulged out of her head when she saw the leaderboard. Not only had one of the trophies been found, but it was the Stealth trophy! And it had been located by . . . *Ray Fong*? Not seven minutes into the game, and already her goal of being the first student since Agent 4 to collect all the trophies was ruined.

She couldn't help but smile, though. Clearly, she'd underestimated her competition—maybe this was going to be a challenge, after all. And there was nothing Tanya liked more than a challenge. . . .

Mostly because she usually won.

The librarian never even looked up as Tanya quietly made her way to the back of the building. Despite the sign, the elevator door opened easily at her touch. Tanya ducked inside and hit the DOOR CLOSE button. Only once she was safely hidden from any prying eyes did she take a moment to breathe and consider the situation.

The elevator was a featureless silver box, with no possible place to hide anything, even something as small as a trophy. Judging from the layer of dust, no one other than Sensei had used this elevator in a long time. There were six buttons set into a panel on the left side of the door. The first was marked GROUND, and clearly represented the floor she was on. The rest were labeled s1 through s5.

It wasn't hard to figure out where Sensei had gone. The buttons labeled s1 through s4 were still covered in a layer of dirt, but GROUND and s5 had been rubbed clean. Tanya took a deep breath and steadied herself for whatever was to come.

"The peaceful warrior is the prepared warrior," she whispered. It was one of Sensei's mantras. Tanya waited until her heart had slowed to its normal pace. Then she pushed s5.

Three seconds later, the doors dinged open. Tanya launched herself into a dive, rolling out of the elevator and into a pitch-black room. She came to her feet right as a flood of brilliant lights turned on, blinding her. Frantically, she threw herself to one side, hoping to dodge the trap she had just blundered into. Instead, she slammed shoulder first into something very large and very heavy.

"Ow!" she yelped involuntarily. *There goes the element of surprise,* she thought. Her eyes had adapted to the light, and she realized she was pressed against the edge of a large metal bookshelf. She spun around, placing the bookshelf at her back, and prepared to fight her opponent.

But there was no one. The elevator had spit her out into a narrow hallway that seemed to run along one side of a GINORMOUS room. Floor-to-ceiling metal bookshelves ran in parallel rows away from her, perpendicular to the wall that had the elevator. Her back was to one of them, and she was facing the now-closed elevator doors. But there wasn't a person to be seen.

They were toying with her, she realized. They had her trapped. She knew if she tried to go back upstairs, they would come at her from behind while she waited for the elevator doors to open. Having this bookcase at her back was the safest place she could be. Her heart was hammering in her chest, but she forced herself to stay still. The room was quiet, and cold, and very, very creepy. It looked like the kind of place that nightmares went when they wanted to be scared.

A minute later, the lights went out again. Tanya ducked, certain an attack was coming, but the lights flashed back on to reveal a room just as empty as it had been moments before.

It's a motion detector! she realized. This part of the library was so rarely used, it made sense to leave all the lights off unless someone was down here. She laughed at her own fears.

Now that she knew she wouldn't have to fight Sensei at a moment's notice, Tanya took some time to look around. Each row of shelves was outfitted with a small black dial. Curious, Tanya turned one.

With a low buzzing sound, lights flickered on down the length of the aisle. The dial was a timer! Once you left the main hallway, Tanya realized, the rest of the lights weren't on motion detectors. Instead, the knobs controlled the lights for the aisles. Already the one she'd tested was beginning to run down. Judging from the size and speed of the knob, one turn would give her about fifteen minutes of light. That meant she had to act fast.

Once again, it was easy to follow Sensei's tracks. Tanya walked down to the aisle to her left, where Sensei's footprints left the main hallway and went off into the darkness. Carefully, Tanya flattened herself against the nearest bookcase and turned the knob. The lights came on, and nothing happened. Tanya counted to ten, then peeked her head out. There were just books and dusty footprints as far as the eye could see. All the way at the end of the aisle she could just barely make out a small door. She turned the light knob all the way, ensuring that she had the full fifteen minutes. Then she set off at a dead run down the corridor.

Tanya had only gone about twenty feet before something slammed into the back of her head so hard she flew forward and landed on her stomach. Her Martial Arts training took over, and she instinctively rolled to the side as she landed, trying to avoid whoever had ambushed her. On her back, she cocked her legs in a defensive kicking position—but again no one was there! All she saw was a heavy hardcover book on the floor by her head. She grabbed the fallen book. If worse came to worse, she could use it as a shield.

"I know you're out there!" she yelled. Sensei must have stationed some student Helpers among the shelves, to slow down the Hunters. But it would take more than a few first-years tossing textbooks to slow Tanya down.

When no one responded, Tanya carefully rose to a defensive crouch. Before she could fully stand, another book came flying right above her head!

"Hey!" she yelled, spinning around to spot her opponent. As she did, another book hit her in the arm so hard it went numb below the elbow! This one had come from the opposite direction. Was her enemy on the move? Or was there more than one of them? Either way, she wasn't in a good position.

Tanya decided she had to get out of the hall-way. She rolled to her feet and started sprinting toward the door, but within seconds the air was filled with flying books. There were too many for her to dodge. They beat her backward, step by step. She retreated to the very entrance of the aisle. There, the onslaught stopped. Eager to catch her opponents, she ran to the aisle that was parallel to this one, certain she would find a few of the blue-shirted Helpers waiting for her.

Tanya had just a momentary impression of movement in an empty hallway before the lights went out again.

"Argh!" she yelled with frustration. In the dark, she fumbled around for the dial. By the time the light came back, there was nothing to see. Quickly, she checked all of the rows of bookshelves, but found no one.

The hairs on the back of Tanya's neck stood up. She had seen a lot of strange things in her time at St. Perfidious. But had Sensei actually managed to find a ghost for her to fight?

Tanya smiled. If so, Sensei was in for a surprise. Tanya's favorite movie was *Poltergeist*, and no disembodied spirit was going to stop her. She followed Sensei's footprints once again, this time keeping a close eye on the books. Suddenly, she heard a whisper of movement behind her. She spun around just in time to see a book flying at her face.

"Haaae-ya!" she yelled, snapping her hand out in a powerful swinging blow, using her book-shield as a bat. The book careened off to the side. As she watched, the hole in the shelf where the book had been was filled by an identical yellow book—which itself came flying at her two seconds later. This time she ducked, and it sailed over her head and down the hallway. In its wake, three other books shot out of the walls.

She stepped back a foot and watched the spot where the first book had been. Yet again, another book filled its place on the shelf. But this time, it stayed still.

An idea was forming in Tanya's head. She reached out and swung her arm through the air. Sure enough, the first book launched.

They must be on motion sensors as well! she realized. This whole place was one giant automated booby trap. And judging from the bruises that were rising on her arm, it was a very good booby trap.

Tanya thought for a moment. The bookshelves went all the way up to the ceiling, and all the way over to the opposite wall. There was no way to get to the door except by going through this hall. Barreling down it hadn't worked—there were simply too many book-a-pults shooting at her. She looked at the book in her hand, the one that had hit her in the head. She threw it down the hallway as hard as she could. Within seconds, a hailstorm of books was flying at it. It looked as though the hallway were the center of a tiny tornado.

The book-a-pults were so fast that there was no way she could get down the hall before they had reloaded. But she couldn't just run through them, either. While she thought, she pulled another book off the shelf and tossed it down the aisle. The same books fired from the same places at the same time. That meant there was a pattern. And if there was a pattern, she could learn it!

It took five more tosses, but soon Tanya had memorized the series. There were forty-seven book-a-pults total: twenty-two on her left, and twenty-five on her right. She took a deep breath and set off down the hall, ducking, diving, and pirouetting her way past flying books. They fired faster and faster, but they couldn't touch Tanya. In less than a minute, she was down the hall and through the door. The silver cube sat on a tiny wooden table waiting for her.

Dong!

CHAPTER FIVE

Ray was so excited as he left the quad that he couldn't help but skip, something he hadn't done since he was a little kid. He, Ray Fong, had found the first trophy of the Hunt! And not only that, but he now held a school record! He'd never even gotten the highest score on a test, and now students would remember his name for years to come.

This first touch of success electrified Ray, and now he was determined to find the other trophies. As he slowed down to a walk, he started to make a plan. The other Hunters had been waiting for this day for weeks, if not months. He had to outsmart them. But how?

He sat down in the shade of a big oak tree near the building that contained the entrance to the real St. Perfidious. It was funny to think that just a few hours ago he'd been jogging around the campus, looking at all the plants, imagining a relaxed and easy afternoon. Now here he was, in first place!

Dong!

Well, make that tied for first place, Ray thought as he checked his WATCH. Tanya had claimed the Martial Arts trophy. Ray wasn't surprised—Tanya was one tough spy. He didn't know if he could beat her, but he was ready to take a shot at it!

With two trophies already found, Ray had to make some quick decisions. There was no point in going after the Strategy trophy. It was always the last one. And if Ray had a weakness, it was definitely Tech. So that left Disguise.

M. Masque was such a master of illusion that he had once perfectly transformed an ordinary bunny into a velociraptor, which had been really funny until a terrified second-year called the National Guard. In M. Masque's hands, the trophy could be anything. Ray was going to need a clue. With nothing else to go on, he went inside, grabbed the hidden elevator in the third-floor bathroom, and headed to Professor Masque's Disguise laboratory.

Imagine the biggest, craziest closet you've ever seen. Now imagine bigger. Crazier. That was the Disguise lab. Rumor had it that there were over forty thousand complete costumes in the room. But M. Masque kept it neat and orderly. In the center was a small group of desks, each with a mirror, a light, and a portable changing room next to it. The rest of the room was racks and boxes of clothing, organized by a ridiculously complex system that none of the students could ever follow.

Ray could tell from the moment he arrived that other Hunters had been there first. The differences were subtle, but Ray noticed those kinds of things. The desks were in neat rows—but none of them quite matched up with the yellow-tiled floor. And while none of the clothing looked out of order, Ray had already noticed not one, but two pockets that had been flipped inside out, as though someone had rifled through them in a hurry. Professor Masque would never let that stand.

"Well, well. If it isn't my competition!"

Ray whirled around to find Tanya leaning in the doorway. Though they'd shared a few classes, they'd never really talked before. For a second, he was shocked at the change in her appearance, but then he figured it out—she'd been wearing a wig all year! Now, that was commitment to a disguise. He couldn't help but be impressed.

"Hi, Tanya!" he said, sticking out his hand to shake hers. She let it hang there awkwardly.

"Good job on the Martial Arts trophy," Ray tried again. From the look of the bruises on her, getting that trophy couldn't have been easy.

Tanya nodded, and one—one hundredth of a smile appeared on her face. "Thanks," she replied. She was already looking past Ray, scanning the rest of the room. She must have seen the same little details Ray had noticed, because her smile slipped away. She seemed to have forgotten Ray was there at all.

So much for making some friends during this, Ray thought to himself as Tanya walked back out of the room. At the last second, she turned back.

"You did pretty good yourself," she said

grudgingly. Then she smiled. "But I'm still going to beat you!"

"Bring it!" Ray yelled as Tanya ran out of the room. He clapped his hand over his mouth. He couldn't believe he'd said that! Trash-talking wasn't like him. But he had to admit, he kind of enjoyed it.

Suddenly, he heard other voices from the hallway. Without thinking about it, he dived into one of the portable changing rooms. It was simple instinct—he was a spy, he needed information, and people were on their way. Chances were the voices belonged to other Hunters, who'd made their way here for the same reason Ray had. If he was lucky, they might let slip some useful information.

Quickly, it became obvious that these weren't Hunters. Instead, they were two of M. Masque's Helpers, neither of whom was particularly happy to be working on the day of the Hunt.

"I can't believe how much stuff he needed us to buy!" grumbled one. Ray heard a dragging sound, and guessed that Professor Masque had sent them to put his room back in order. He grinned to himself. At least *some* things about Professor Masque were predictable!

"It couldn't have been that much," said a second voice. "Look at all this stuff! How much more could he need?"

"Dude, the list was as long as my arm."

A honking laugh came from the other side of the room.

"Yeah, right."

"For serious! Look!"

"Wow, that is a lot of stuff!"

"Long as my arm, right?"

Suddenly, Ray was certain that the list was the key to finding the Disguise trophy. But how was he going to get it? It was against the rules to interfere with the Helpers, so he had to find some way to trick them. He wracked his brain, but as the Helpers finished cleaning the room and left, his shoulders drooped with despair. This was his big chance, and he was blowing it.

He stepped out from inside the changing room and looked up at the pictures of Professor Masque. There he was disguised as an astronaut, there as a dog, there as a dining-room table. . . . His (or maybe her?) skill at disguise knew no bounds. Professor Masque could literally be anything.

That was it! Professor Masque could be anything, which meant . . . *anything could be Professor Masque!*

Ray grabbed clothing almost at random, pulling things off the racks until finally he found a giant poncho that would cover his entire body. He dived into the boxes of props and pulled out a sombrero, giant pink sunglasses, and a bushy fake wig with a matching mustache. It wasn't the best disguise he'd ever made, but no one could tell who was beneath it.

As he exited the room, he heard the sound of an elevator door closing farther down the hallway. From the lit call button, he could tell the Helpers were headed up. Poncho flapping, Ray raced up the emergency stairs to cut them off.

He was winded by the time he got to the top floor, but he beat the elevator by two seconds. As it opened, two shocked Helpers stared out at the crazy, panting poncho man in front of them.

Just sound like you know what you're talking about, Ray told himself.

"So, is my classroom back in order?" he asked. He made no effort to disguise his voice. He didn't know either of these Helpers, and if his voice sounded strange to them, they'd just put it down to being part of his—or rather, M. Masque's—disguise.

"Yes, sir!" the two Helpers responded immediately. Now that they thought they were talking to Professor Masque, they straightened up and tried their best to look happy about the jobs they had been given.

"Excellent!" said Ray. Did M. Masque say "excellent"? Had he just given himself away? Ray had to fight back the urge to panic. Luckily, the students were so used to seeing M. Masque take on different personas, they didn't give it a second thought.

"I have one more important task for you," said Ray. "The shopping list I gave you yesterday? I need it back. Can't let it fall into the wrong hands, you know?"

With a nod, the girl on his left unzipped her backpack and gave him the list. Ray snatched it from her hand and stared at it. He was so distracted he almost forgot the two Helpers were still there.

"Uhhh . . . and I need you to do three other things," he mumbled. "Get me a . . . uhh . . . a velveteen rabbit, three feet of gold wire, and the largest rubber-band ball you can find."

Ray figured that would keep them too busy to go report back to the real Professor Masque. But the longer he spoke, the more he could feel his mustache beginning to slide off. Quickly he turned away from the Helpers and hopped on the elevator. As the door closed, he heard the girl say something to the boy about how strange he seemed to be behaving. But he had the list now, so even if they figured out that he wasn't M. Masque, it was too late to stop him.

To his surprise, the list included almost no clothing or makeup. Instead, it all seemed to be gardening supplies! He headed aboveground, shedding pieces of his disguise as he went. He felt sweaty and gross but excited. As he read down the list, he felt more and more certain that Professor Masque had hidden his trophy somewhere on the grounds.

Two items on the list caught Ray's attention. The first was twenty-four white petunias. The second was one red petunia. Something about that tickled his mind, but he couldn't say what it was. As he made his way out onto the quad again, he was surprised to see that the sun was high in the sky. Checking his WATCH, he was shocked to find it was two twenty p.m.! Where had the day gone? Could it really have been seven hours since he'd jogged this very path?

Jogging! That was it. That was why that list of flowers sounded familiar. He'd watched a gardener plant those petunias this morning! The gardener been putting them in a square around the big WELCOME sign to St. Perfidious Academy. It must have been M. Masque!

There were other people around, and in the distance, Ray could hear the whirring of Lisa's mini-motor scooter. So he made himself walk slowly down the path toward the entrance to the school. He tried his best to hide his excitement and look sad and lost. The last thing he wanted was for another Hunter to follow him and steal the trophy away.

"Hey, Ray, good job, man!" shouted a girl from across the quad. Ray didn't even know her name, but he nodded, smiled, and waved. It felt good to suddenly be somebody at school.

Ten agonizingly slow minutes later, Ray finally arrived at the bed of white petunias he had seen that morning. Sure enough, a single red flower sat at the very center. Ray ran right in and began digging with his bare hands. In the dark wet soil beneath the red petunia's roots, something silver gleamed.

Dong!

CHAPTER SIX

Tanya couldn't help but smile when the gong sounded this time. She knew it was Ray even before she checked her WATCH. She would never, ever tell Eric, but this was the most fun she'd had in years! She was the kind of spy who researched her opponents endlessly. She couldn't remember the last time someone had surprised her. Getting one trophy, even as fast as Ray had done it, could have been blind luck. This second trophy meant he was serious business. But so long as Tanya got the remaining two, she could come out on top. And she *always* came out on top.

Her plan for capturing the Tech trophy was pretty simple. Dr. O was, like, Spock-level logical—the kind of guy who made detailed to-do lists every day, with "Make a To-Do List" as the first entry on the list. But he was also very, very absentminded. Six years ago, he'd forgotten where he'd hidden the Tech trophy, and it had been found only by accident. Where would a logical but forgetful person hide something? In a place they knew well. Since Dr. O spent about 95 percent of his time in the computer lab, Tanya figured she'd start there.

Tanya submitted her eye to a retinal scan outside of the computer lab. Dr. O was always working on ways to improve school security. A soft blue light shone in her eye for a few seconds, and then the doors whooshed open. A quiet voice spoke in her left ear.

"Welcome, Tanya. You have a sty forming in your right eye. Enjoy the computer lab."

Dr. O must have hooked the scanner up to do eye exams as well. *Cool!* thought Tanya, though she wasn't happy to hear about her eye. Tanya expected to get just as perfect scores in her eye exams as she did on all her other tests.

The computer lab was the only place on campus that seemed to be business as usual. Inside the dark, cool room four or five students were busy typing away. Oddly, they were all wearing elaborate headsets that hid their faces.

Wiz-Kids, thought Tanya. *I'm not surprised.*

The "Wiz-Kids" was what everyone at St. Perfidious called the Tech-focused students. And "focused" was definitely the right word for them. They wouldn't even leave the computer lab for the Hunt—

Tanya broke off mid-thought. She'd been so busy looking at the other students that she hadn't noticed the trophy! It was sitting right in the middle of the room in a shaft of silver light. She ran for it, shocked that none of her competitors had found it yet.

"Score!" she yelled, as she grabbed the trophy. But her glove passed right through it!

The hologram of the trophy shattered into a million points of light. When they re-formed, it was in the shape of Dr. O.

"Tsk, tsk!" he said, staring right at Tanya. "You didn't think it would be that easy, did you? This year's Tech trophy has gone digital, and if you expect to win it, so will you."

The hologram of Dr. O pointed to a row of computer desks. Now that Tanya was paying attention, she could see that the other people in the lab were all other Hunters — which meant they had a lead on her! Quickly, she raced over to one of the unclaimed monitors. The screen had a single icon on it: a gleaming silver cube. She double-tapped it. For a second, nothing happened. Then the screen began to swirl in a hypnotic spiral.

"Welcome, Hunter Jones." The computer spoke with the same woman's voice that had checked her eyes. "Please put on your virtual-reality mask and prepare to enter the Hunt."

A large headpiece sat next to the computer, and Tanya impatiently pulled it on. She had no idea how far behind the other players she was, and she wanted to get on with it. The headset left her blind and deaf, completely unable to make out anything from the real world.

"This will allow you to see the playing field," the woman's voice continued. "Your glove can interact with objects in the virtual world. Blue balloons are power-ups. Red balloons activate the game's built-in security systems. I recommend you steer well clear of them. The first Hunter who can hold the trophy for five consecutive minutes wins."

The world inside Tanya's headpiece began to take shape. Slowly, light appeared. Then sound. She seemed to be in a virtual version of the school gym—the exact same one where she and Eric had fought this morning. As the world became more real, the woman's voice became fainter and fainter. Tanya barely heard her final words.

"Good luck. You'll need it."

Tanya was momentarily blinded by a flash of white light. Before she could recover, she sensed something big coming her way from behind. She dived to the side, rolling over one shoulder and landing some ten feet away from where she had started.

Brrooom!!

Something large exploded behind her. The shock wave knocked her to her knees. Her vision was clearing now. The virtual gym had been turned into a giant war zone. A paintball war zone, to be exact. The area where she'd landed had been blanketed by the hot-pink contents of a giant hand grenade. But even as she watched, the paint was fading. Clouds of smoke drifted across the landscape, obscuring most of it from view, but she could make out enough details to tell that it had the same general layout as the real gym. But there were more obstacles now: added trenches, half-collapsed buildings, and small towers that were perfect for snipers.

This is going to be fun! Tanya thought.

Far off in the distance, she saw three Hunters in a pitched shoot-out. She wondered where they had gotten their guns, but a moment later, a blue light appeared to her left, and she remembered the instructions she'd been given. *Blue means power-up!* she reminded herself. She grabbed at the glowing ball with her left hand, but it passed right through.

"What?" she wondered, before she remembered that only her glove could interact with things in the computer world. She grabbed it again, properly this time, and removed her hand to find herself holding a slingshot and a bag of bright green pebbles. Not the best weapon she could have gotten, but it was a start.

Dong!

For a second, Tanya was afraid she was too late and someone had already claimed the Tech trophy, but this was a different sound. Dr. O's voice filled the room.

"Erica Khatri has the trophy! The countdown begins now."

In the corner of her vision, a small digital counter appeared. But it disappeared just as quickly.

"Looks like she's lost it, folks! The trophy is back up for grabs."

Tanya smiled.

"Not for long!" she yelled.

CHAPTER SEVEN

Argh!" yelled Ray, as the virtual world dissolved away from him, spitting him back into Dr. O's lab. It was the third time in less than five minutes that he'd been tagged out. He ripped off his goggles and threw them down on the desk. The other Hunters, covered in their headpieces, didn't even notice. Ray was so frustrated he could scream.

Going to Professor Masque's classroom had worked out pretty well for him, so Ray had decided to follow the same strategy with Dr. O—but so far, the results hadn't been promising. He'd been completely fooled by the hologram, and was only thankful that none of the other Hunters had been able to see him fall flat on his face when he tried to grab it. Following the instructions, he'd logged into the game, but he found it nearly impossible to understand. Before he could even get his bearings, he kept finding himself covered in paint! And every time he was hit, the game shut down, forcing him to lose precious time as he logged back on.

Ray never liked video games. Somehow, despite knowing how to do all sorts of cool spy stuff in the real world, he couldn't figure out how to do any of it with a controller in his hand. His seven-year-old sister routinely beat him in just about every game there was. So this Tech challenge was his worst nightmare, for real. It didn't help that all the other Hunters had a head start, and got to watch him fail over and over again.

And Ray really meant *all* the other Hunters. With only the Strategy and Tech trophies left, everyone was logged into Dr. O's arena. Ray suspected he might have a target on his back because of the other trophies, but it wasn't until he started playing that he realized how big that target was.

"Maybe I should just leave," Ray said to himself. He could get started on the Strategy trophy. It was always the last one found, but it didn't seem like anyone was going to get the Tech trophy anytime soon. Maybe he could surprise everyone once again! Anything would be better than logging back in just to die again. The resulting burst of static every time he got shot was beginning to give him a headache.

Ray rubbed his eyes and looked around at all the other players, hard at work. If all of the other Hunters were here, wasn't he making a mistake by leaving? Didn't they know best? They all had plans and strategies. He was just making it up as he went along.

WWHBD, Ray thought to himself. *What would Headmaster Booker do?*

Of course, if he could figure that out, he wouldn't be at St. Perfidious—he'd be a spy already!

Ray stood up, hesitated, and then sat back down. Then he stood up again. Then he sat down. He put on the goggles; then he took them off. Then he put them on again. Then he took them off and stood up.

Stop it! he told himself. This was just wasting time. He had to be logical. As far as he could tell, he had two choices: Log into the game and try for the Tech trophy, or leave and look for the Strategy one.

As he gazed out at all the other Hunters, a third option occurred to him.

"Ha!" Ray laughed out loud as he thought about it. Rarely did he think of himself as a brilliant strategist. But maybe trying to channel Headmaster Booker had fired up some crafty part of his mind.

This is going to be fun, he thought as he logged in for the ninth and, hopefully, final time.

Four seconds later he was back out of the game again—a new personal low. It took three more tries before Ray managed to get into the game and not get killed instantly. Luckily, on his last attempt, he appeared in the game in a now mostly collapsed version of the school's gym.

Peering out the window, he could see a giant battle happening not fifteen feet from where he stood. While he had been logged out, Ken Cohen must have grabbed the trophy, and, judging by the clock in the upper corner of Ray's vision, he'd managed to hold on to it for almost four minutes. Soon, he would be declared the winner.

But not if Ray had anything to say about it. With all the Hunters in one place, this was the perfect opportunity.

Carefully, Ray snuck out of his hiding hole.

Splat!

A giant splotch of green paint appeared just a few feet from Ray's head. He dived, fearing the worst, but no more shots followed. Apparently, everyone had bigger things to worry about. The countdown clock now stood at fifty-three seconds.

Ray scanned the edges of the arena, looking for that elusive glow. The blue orbs were tagged as fast as they appeared, since every Hunter was looking for an edge over the others. But Ray didn't care about them. His strategy depended on the red orbs, the dangerous ones. Forty feet away, he spotted the telltale red glow leaking out from inside a rubber ball. A hundred feet farther down, there was another sitting on the ground, and then a cluster of two floating in the air by the wall.

There were only forty seconds left. It was now or never.

Ray put his head down and ran. At any moment, he expected to be blown out of the game. But he made it to the first orb with no problems. He took a moment to figure out the best route to the next orb, then tagged the first one and took off running.

An electronic roar filled the room. Ray turned back to see the orb growing into a giant red dragon. It was pixilated like a cartoon, but Ray had no doubt those teeth meant business.

He didn't even pause to tag the next one; he just ran through it. This one exploded on contact, and for a second, Ray thought his sabotage plan was over before it had even really begun. But the glowing red pieces didn't seem to hurt him. Instead, they floated in the wind, seemingly harmless. But as Ray ran toward the last two red orbs, the little pieces began to land. As each one hit the ground, a four-foot-tall red "toy" soldier appeared. Ray was certain that their plastic guns shot real paint pellets.

The countdown clock suddenly disappeared

from Ray's screen. He risked a glance back, and saw the dragon raking paint-fire across the other Hunters.

That ought to slow them down, he thought as he jumped for the last two orbs. He got one, which seemed to open hidden gun windows all around the gym. He was leaping for the second when something hit him hard in the back. He was already disappearing from the game as he twisted around to see Tanya standing there, looking angry (but also impressed, Ray thought).

As he took off his headpiece, Ray heard surprised and angry exclamations all around the computer lab. His plan had worked. The trophy was back up for grabs, and with all the chaos he'd created, he doubted anyone would be claiming it soon.

On his way out the door, he flipped off the light switch, plunging the lab into darkness. Just one more way to keep everyone busy.

Ray'd bought himself some time. Now he just had to figure out what to do with it.

CHAPTER SIX

*W*hen I get my hands on Ray . . . thought Tanya, as she hurled one of the toy soldiers into another. The two exploded in a shower of sparks, but Tanya wasn't paying attention to them anymore. She had thirty seconds to go before the Tech trophy was all hers. She just had two small problems—Kim and Ken Cohen.

Make that three small problems, Tanya thought as a dark shadow spread over her. That darn dragon was the biggest danger. It was a dirty trick Ray had pulled, but it was also very smart. The Hunters, all intent on claiming the trophy, had been taken completely by surprise. The dragon's virtual fire breath had booted everyone from the game at the same time. When they logged back in, the arena was overrun with angry little red men and carefully hidden guns that tracked them with motion sensors. And above it all circled the dragon.

Twenty-five seconds were left on her count-down. She was so close she could almost taste it. She looked up at her goal: the pillar where she had started her day. Or at least, the virtual version of the one she had hidden atop this morning, waiting for Eric.

Tanya felt, more than heard, someone firing at her from close range. Instinctively she zigzagged. The pillar in front of her was quickly covered with orange and blue paint splatters—the Cohen twins were right behind her. The shadow of the dragon was getting smaller and darker, which meant it was diving toward her. It figured: All of her enemies were coming at once.

If that wasn't exactly what Tanya had been counting on, she might have been afraid.

Tanya had been the first one back in the game after the dragon had killed them all, and so she saw Ray activate the other defense systems. She didn't know how many red orbs he had managed to tag before she shot him, but it was enough. The first few minutes back in the game were complete chaos, before Lisa Terrington had gotten the Hunters to agree on a temporary truce. For fifteen minutes, they ignored the gleaming silver trophy and worked together to destroy as many of the traps as they could. They made short work of most of the little red men and the motion-sensing guns, but the dragon seemed untouchable. Nothing they did even scratched its scales. After their fifteen minutes of cooperation was over, the Hunters were back on one another's tails. Tanya had lucked into a blue power-up orb that made her 20 percent faster than everyone else, and she'd annihilated the competition. Securing the trophy had almost been a breeze, and in just a matter of seconds, she'd have a second win under her belt and be back after Ray.

"Get her, Ken!"

Tanya heard Kim scream behind her. Without looking, Tanya fired her paint pistol in the general direction of Kim's voice. She slowed down as she did it. She needed to keep them close—just not too close.

Fifteen seconds left. She was almost there. Tanya heard the dragon drawing in its breath, getting ready to roast them all. She had to time this perfectly. The pillar was no more than twenty feet away.

Ten seconds.

Now! Tanya thought, as she jumped. She turned in midair so that her feet hit the pillar first. She kicked off with her left leg, sending her tucked body spiraling through into the very same trench she'd tricked Eric into before. The impact hurt, but she flattened herself against the bottom of the hole.

And not a moment too soon—the air above her was suddenly filled with roaring flames. From the shouting, she knew the dragon had gotten Kim and Ken, but it passed over her without even singeing her virtual hair.

She stood up and counted down with the clock. "Three, two, one."

Above her head, the dragon exploded into fireworks! Tanya couldn't help but gasp, even though none of it was real. Instead of going out, the fiery particles in the air seemed to move with a mind of their own, until they spelled out her name in glittering light.

DONG!

The sound of the virtual gong and the real gong merged into one as Tanya left the virtual arena behind. She took off her headset. Around her, the other Hunters were all leaving the game, giving her looks that were equal parts admiration and envy. Tanya was used to that.

She had two trophies. Ray had two trophies. One of them was going to win. As far as Tanya was concerned, no one else was left in this game. She had only one strategy: Find Ray and stick to him like glue. If he went to the tennis courts, she would go to the tennis courts. If he blew his nose, so would she. She'd be as close to him as his shadow. There'd be no way he could find the trophy without her knowing.

So long as he isn't finding it right now, Tanya thought to herself as she jogged out of the computer lab. She quickly checked her WATCH. It was close to four in the afternoon. Her stomach growled painfully. She hadn't eaten a thing since breakfast, but now wasn't the time for that.

With almost all the Hunters in the same place, it didn't take long to flip through the school security cameras on her WATCH and find Ray. He was sitting in the main quad, right by the statue of Headmaster Booker. If he was on the verge of finding the final trophy, he was doing a pretty good job of hiding it.

Tanya ran right up to the edge of the quad, slowing down before she got within sight. She checked her WATCH to make sure Ray hadn't moved. Judging from the security camera, it looked as though she could get within ten feet of him if she crept up from behind, going from bush to bush.

It took twenty minutes to make her way the four hundred feet that separated her from Ray. She had just achieved her final position, hidden in the shade of a mulberry bush not seven feet from the statue of Headmaster Booker, when Ray suddenly leaped to his feet.

"Finally," Ray said. "I've been waiting for you."

CHAPTER NINE

As Ray had closed the door on Dr. O's computer lab, something occurred to him.

He really, really wanted to win this.

He didn't want to do well. He didn't want to impress the teachers, or do better than he thought he would, or do his best. He wanted to *win*.

Ray had never thought much about winning before. He was that guy who was content to work hard and leave it at that. But with two trophies in his grasp and only one left unaccounted for, winning the Hunt was suddenly an achievable dream. There was only one student left who could beat him: Tanya Jones. As she had shown throughout the Hunt, she was a smart, tough competitor. Ray wasn't really sure he could beat her in a direct competition. But he knew she wanted to win just as badly as he did. . . .

Gears started turning in Ray's head, and by the time he had reached the elevator, he had a plan. Quickly, he headed to the quad. Agent 4 was sitting at the judges' table, sorting through some papers. She smiled and nodded when he approached. M. Masque was with her, still dressed as a robot. The other teachers were nowhere to be seen.

Ray took a seat in the shadow of the statue of Headmaster Booker and waited. He knew Tanya would come to him. She wanted to win, and the only way to ensure that Ray didn't get the trophy was to keep tabs on him. This was the safest, most neutral place he could think to meet her, since the judges' table was right within eyesight.

And so he waited. And waited. And waited.

Eventually, after what seemed like hours (but was probably only fifteen minutes), he heard a rustling in the mulberry tree to his left. Ray leaped to his feet.

"Finally," Ray said. "I've been waiting for you."

He walked over to the quivering bush. When he got within a foot of it, a terrified squirrel launched itself at him.

"Ha!" laughed Ray. Seemed like his spying instincts weren't quite as good as he thought.

Twice more Ray yelled at the wildlife, but on his fourth attempt, Tanya strode boldly out from behind the mulberry.

"How did you know I was there?" she asked.

Ray smiled. "I have my ways," he said.

Tanya stared at him, a smile slowly appearing on her face as she did so. "So you have no idea where the last trophy is, either, huh?"

"Nope," he responded. "You?"

Tanya shook her head. They both sat down on the grass. In the distance, they could hear Lisa's propeller mini-motor scooter, reminding them both that the clock was ticking down.

"You want to win this, right?" said Ray.

Tanya gave him the side eye.

"Right," he said, shaking his head. "Dumb question. Let me try again. We both want to win this, and I have a plan."

"Tell me more," said Tanya. She wasn't sure that any plan Ray came up with would be in her best interest, but she had to admit she didn't have any ideas herself.

"We work together," Ray said. "The only way you don't win this game is if I find the trophy first, and vice versa. So long as we work together, we can tag the trophy at the same time. That way, if we find it, we both win. And if someone else finds it, we *still* both win."

Tanya considered this for a moment. She wasn't used to having to share first place, but Ray had a point.

"How do I know you're not going to cheat and tag the trophy for yourself once we finally find it?" she asked.

Ray stood up. He had anticipated this. He removed his glove.

"Here," he said, holding out his glove in her direction. "If I have on your glove, and you have on mine, whoever tries to steal the trophy will be giving it to the other person!"

Ray was pretty proud of this strategy. It had taken him a while to come up with it, and he felt certain that Headmaster Booker would approve.

Tanya thought about it from every angle, but she couldn't come up with a flaw in his reasoning.

"That's brilliant," she said. "I'm impressed!" She punched Ray playfully in the shoulder. "From now on, I'm going to have to keep a close eye on you. Can't have a spy of your abilities just hanging out in the back of the classroom. We might have to be friends—strictly so I can keep tabs on you, of course."

Ray shook her gloved hand with his, and tried to keep a straight face.

"I agree," he said. "We might have to hang out . . . for professional reasons."

They both laughed. At first, it started off as a chuckle, but every time one of them tried to stop, they'd catch a glimpse of the other and laugh all the harder. It must have been all their nervous energy finally finding a way out.

"So . . ." said Ray, when he could finally speak again. "Where's the last trophy?"

"Darn," she said. "I was hoping you'd know."

"I've heard that it's in the same place every year," Ray said. "But it's also always the hardest trophy to find. How could that be?"

"I watched the tapes of the last ten Hunts," said Tanya. "And they always remove the part where they find the Strategy trophy. But . . ."

Tanya hesitated. Could she really trust Ray? She looked at the shy smile on his quiet face and decided that she wanted to.

"But what?" Ray asked.

"They never seem to be heading in the same direction when they cut the video off. The Hunters, I mean. They're always in some random part of the school, and then suddenly the video just stops."

Ray considered this for a moment.

"So that means . . . the trophy must be inside something that moves!"

Tanya nodded. "That's what I figure. But what?"

Ray opened his mouth—but nothing came out. It could be inside anything, really. A car. A remote-controlled plane. A robot. Heck, it could have been strapped to one of the squirrels he'd yelled at.

Tanya stood up and began pacing around the quad. Ray lay quietly in the shade. They both thought about the trophy.

"What about one of the Helpers?" Tanya said after a while. "Could they have it?"

Ray thought about it.

"No," he finally decided. "Because they might mess up. Headmaster Booker wouldn't leave it to chance like that. What about some kind of robot that moves it around?"

"Too techie," Tanya said firmly. "Headmaster Booker is old-school. He likes less complicated answers."

She sat down heavily at the base of the statue of Headmaster Booker. Right at the exact same moment, Ray rolled up to sitting. They bonked into each other, and Tanya fell backward, lightly dinging her head against the metal coat of the statue. It was an exact replica of the long trench coat Headmaster Booker always wore, right down to the missing third button and the bulging pockets.

Bulging pockets! thought Ray and Tanya simultaneously.

"He has it!" they yelled.

CHAPTER TEN

At the same time, Ray and Tanya looked over at the judges' table—but of course, Headmaster Booker wasn't there. He wouldn't make it that easy!

"Shhh!" said Ray, as Tanya started to talk to him about other places Headmaster Booker might be hiding. He pointed to his ear, and then at the judges. His message was clear: *Let's listen in.*

Tanya caught on instantly. She started a fake quiet conversation with him about lunch, something they could talk about without ever concentrating on it. She leaned in to listen to M. Masque and Agent 4.

"Oh no," said Agent 4. "That's not fair!"

"You're in serious trouble here. I don't see any way for you to get out of this. I'm going to have to remove both of them."

"No!" yelled Tanya, unable to restrain herself. She was so close to winning, they couldn't take her out of the Hunt now.

Agent 4 and M. Masque turned to look at her. Over Agent 4's shoulder, Tanya could make out a game of checkers. M. Masque was about to jump two of Agent 4's pieces.

"No, Ray, I don't think we should take a break for lunch," said Tanya, trying to cover. "Let's go!"

She grabbed Ray and pulled him by the arm, trying to get him away from the judges before he burst out laughing.

"Let's try the headmaster's office instead," suggested Tanya, once Ray had calmed down.

"Doesn't that seem kind of obvious?" asked Ray.

Tanya stared at him.

"Got a better idea?" she asked. Ray shook his head. Together, they headed underground to the headmaster's chambers. His secretary was a very,

very old man named Mingus, who was tall, with dark skin and a low voice like the grumble of a train.

"Not here," he said with a smile. "But something tells me you two are on to his little secret, eh?"

"He has the trophy, right?" said Ray.

"I can't say anything." Mingus smiled. "But I did notice that you two disappeared off the cameras about ten minutes ago. You must be doing something right."

"Yes!" Tanya pumped her fist in the air. They might not have found Headmaster Booker— yet!—but at least now they knew they were definitely on the right track. "You can't tell us where he is, eh?"

"Nope," said Mingus. "I don't even know that myself."

"Does he have any Helpers working with him?" Ray asked, remembering how he'd tricked his way into the Disguise trophy.

Mingus shook his head. "He's alone on this one. You two better get a move on, though. It's getting dark out, and this is going to be a lot harder without any light."

Tanya and Ray took Mingus at his word and set off running. They tried the headmaster's favorite classroom. They tried the apartments where the teachers lived. They tried the cafeteria, the gym, and the teachers' lounge. But Headmaster Booker was nowhere to be found.

"This isn't working," Tanya said, finally. "We need to come up with a plan. Just running around willy-nilly is no way to find the Strategy trophy."

"You're right," said Ray. He sat down in one of the rolling chairs in the teachers' lounge. "But what should we do?"

"Instead of *us* trying to find *him*," Tanya said slowly, "we need *him* to find *us*!"

"Right!" agreed Ray. They stared at each other for a second. "But how do we make that happen?"

And there they were stuck. For ten minutes, they sat thinking in silence. Then Tanya got up and started to pace. Ray started to play with the things on the teachers' desk—pens, pencils, the loudspeaker mic, a broken computer mouse.

"What would make Headmaster Booker appear?" asked Tanya.

"The end of the Hunt," said Ray. "He's always there for that."

"Great," said Tanya. "That helps us not at all."

Ray had said it as a joke, but it made him think.

"Tanya—what if we tricked him somehow? What if we made him think the Hunt was over?"

Tanya stopped pacing and looked at Ray.

"It's a good idea, but it's impossible. He has the last trophy. He'll *know* we didn't win."

"Exactly!" said Ray. "So he'll come to make sure we don't win by cheating."

"Okay," said Tanya, getting into the plan. "But how do we convince him that we've won?"

Ray tapped the microphone on the teachers' desk. "We announce it!"

"Awesome!" said Tanya. "But wait—he'll recognize your voice. Use this!"

Tanya pulled something from her pocket and handed it to Ray. It was a tiny black box.

"What is it?" he asked.

"A voice scrambler," she told him. "I brought it just in case."

"Wow," said Ray. "You really planned for this, didn't you?"

Tanya shrugged, suddenly embarrassed. "Yeah . . . I want to win!"

Ray smiled. "I think I could learn some things from you."

"Back at you," Tanya responded, and punched him in the arm again. "Now, let's do this thing!"

Ray switched on the voice scrambler and then turned on the mic. He leaned forward and tapped it once.

"Testing, testing," he said, trying to sound as official as possible. "We apologize to everyone. There has been a malfunction in the leaderboard system. The final trophy has been discovered by Ray Fong and Tanya Jones. Everyone please report to the main quad so we can declare them the winners."

He switched off the mic and swallowed deeply. "You think it worked?"

"Only one way to find out," said Tanya. "Come on!"

Hand in hand, they ran to the quad. All over campus, students and faculty were leaving their watching places and Hunt parties, and returning to the starting point to celebrate the winners. Tanya and Ray received endless congratulations as they ran. Ray had to admit it felt good, even if they didn't deserve them—yet.

The quad was a giant mess when they arrived. There were students everywhere, and the five teachers were all gathered around the leaderboard scratching their heads.

"I think the answer has just arrived," said Headmaster Booker when he caught sight of Tanya and Ray worming their way through the crowd.

"The two of you have some explaining to do," said Headmaster Booker. "Because as far as we can tell, the leaderboard is working fine."

Tanya let go of Ray's hand and slipped away. Ray stepped forward, getting Headmaster Booker's attention.

"We know," Ray said, speaking slowly to give Tanya the most time possible. "We're not trying to cheat, I promise. We didn't think you'd really believe it."

"Then why did you do it?" asked Headmaster Booker, looking confused.

"To find you," Tanya whispered in his ear. "Gotcha!"

Tanya had snuck up behind Headmaster Booker while Ray distracted him. True to her word, she slipped her ungloved hand into his bulging front left pocket and pulled out a gleaming silver cube. She tossed it high in the air. The entire crowd went silent, watching it flash and sparkle as it spun.

Just as it came within reach, she and Ray jumped. With their gloves, they tagged it at the same moment. A tremendous double *DONG!!* echoed through the quad.

Headmaster Booker looked surprised for a half second, and then he started laughing and applauding at the same time. He leaned in toward the mic on the nearby podium.

"We have a winner—no, we have two winners! Congratulations to Tanya and Ray!"

The crowd went wild. Tanya threw her arm

around Ray and hugged him as hard as she could. Agent 4 was suddenly next to them, a hand on each of their shoulders.

"Well done," she said to the two of them. "You've made me very proud."

Ray looked out over the cheering crowd. For the first time since he'd entered St. Perfidious, he was certain that everyone knew who he was.

ABOUT THE AUTHOR

Hugh Ryan is not a spy, and he totally swears that nothing in this book ever happened to him personally, not even that part where—well, you know. It wasn't him. Nuh-uh. No way. Aside from writing and not being a spy, he loves gardening, spicy tea, terrariums, and taxidermy. Check out his first book in the Spy Academy series, *Mission Twinpossible*.